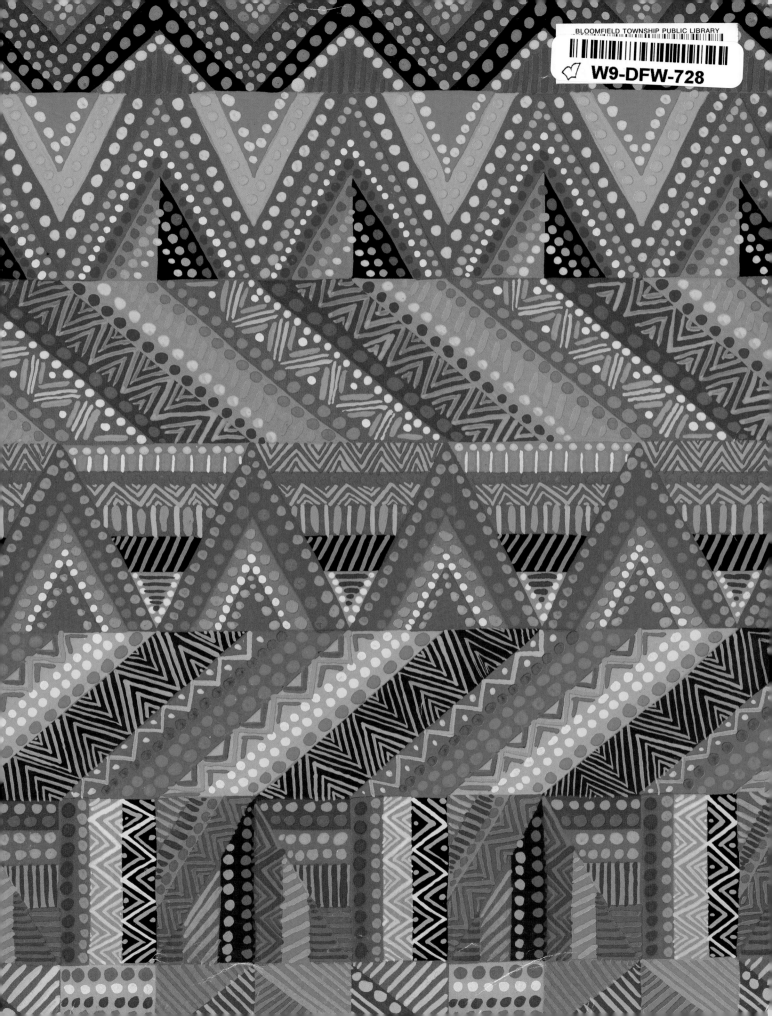

Published by Scholastic Inc.,
730 Broadway, New York, NY 10003, by arrangement with
Oxford University Press.

Library of Congress Cataloging-in-Publication Data

French, Fiona.
King of another country / Fiona French.
p. cm.
Summary: A young African drummer learns the difference between extremes and moderation when the King of the Forest teaches him to say "Yes" instead of "No."
ISBN 0-590-46369-1
[1. Conduct of life—Fiction. 2. Africa—Fiction.] I. Title.
PZ7.F8887Kh 1993
[E]—dc20 92-12661
CIP
AC

12 11 10 9 8 7 6 5 4 3 2 1 3 4 5 6 7 8/9

Printed in Hong Kong

First Scholastic printing, April 1993

Fiona French

King of Another Country

Scholastic Inc.
New York

In an African village
close to the edge of a forest,
there lived a young man called Ojo.
He was not like other people.
Early in the morning when everyone
was asleep, Ojo played the drums.

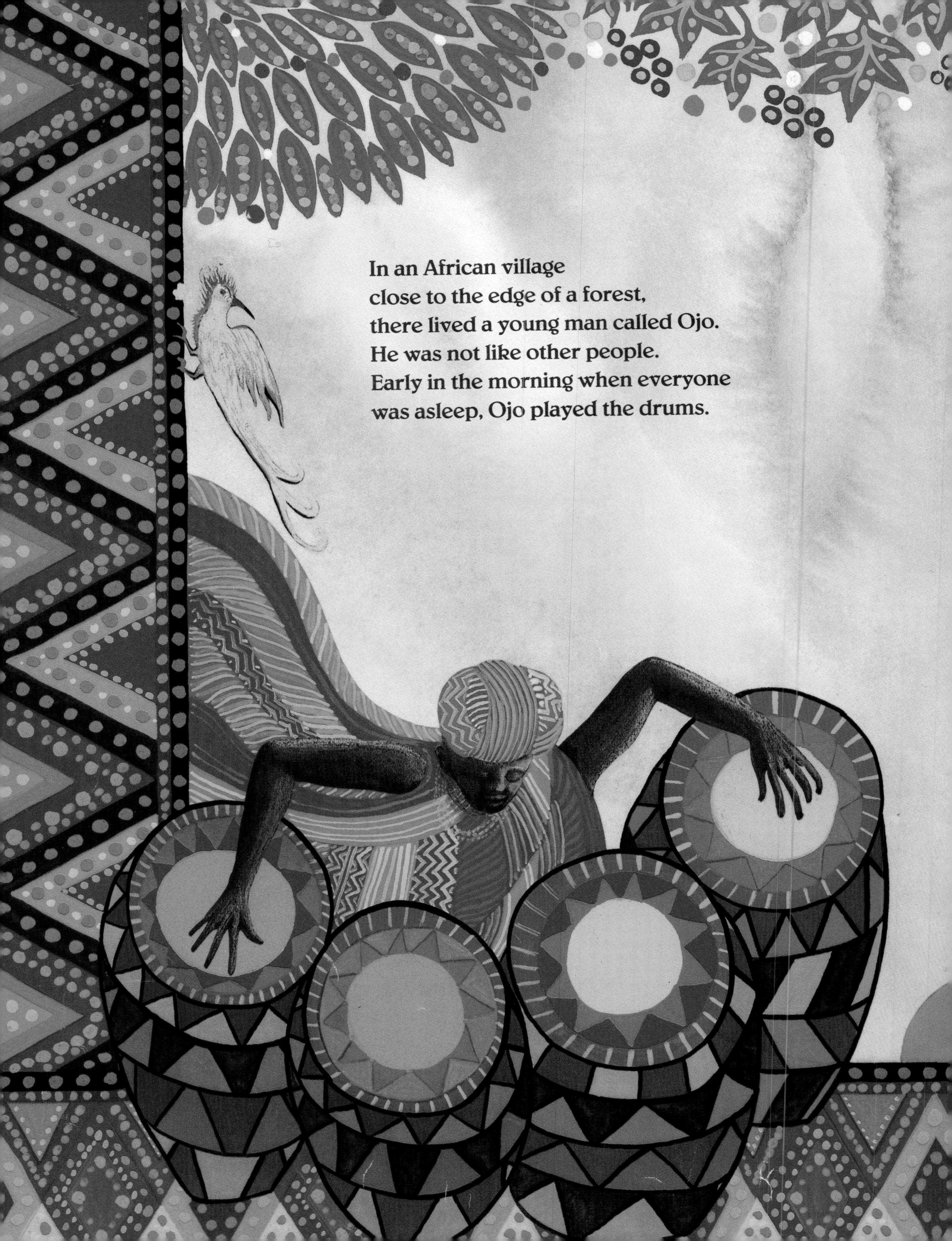

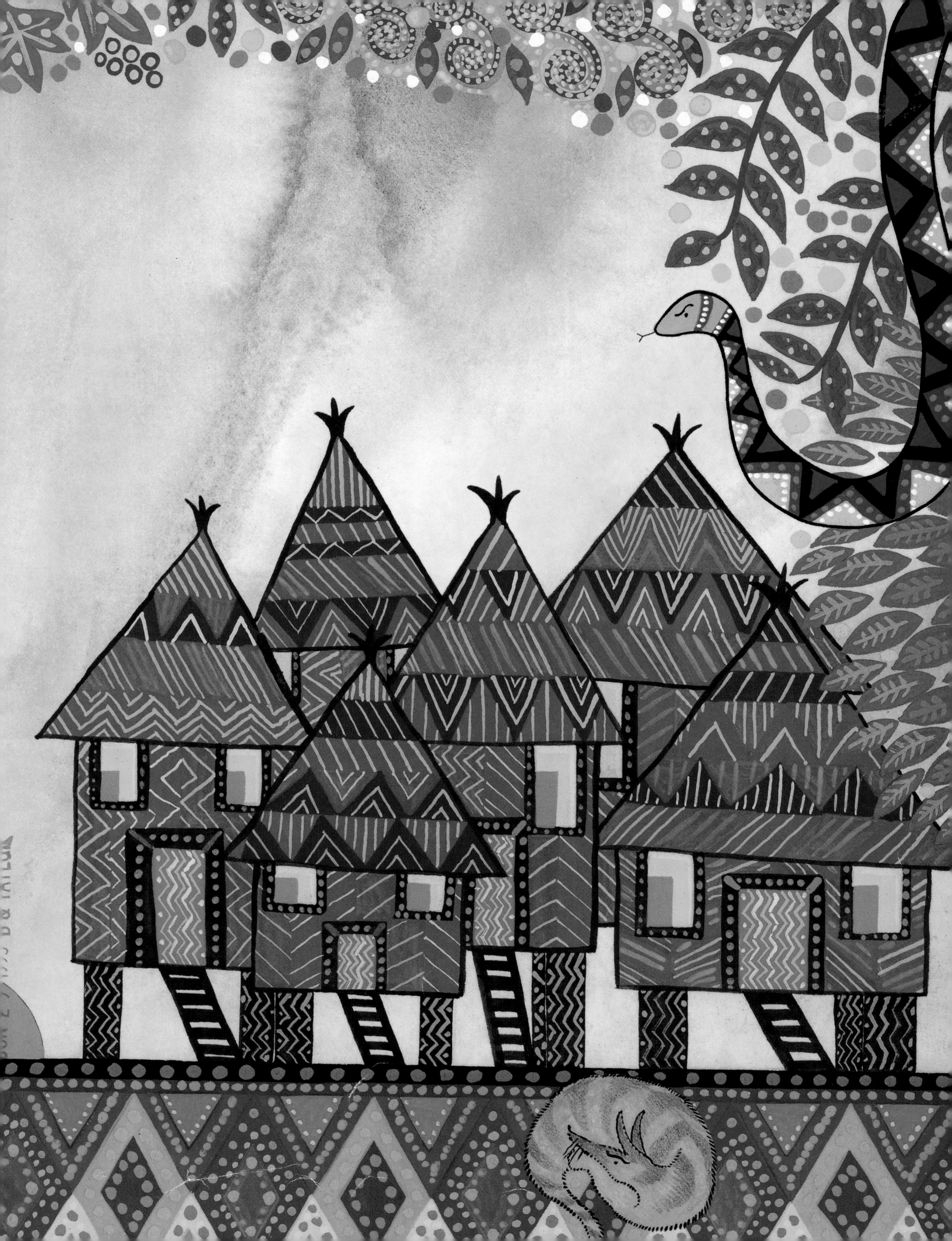

He never helped anyone.
"Ojo, the yams are ripe. Help us bring them in."
"No, I am going off to market."
"Ojo, it is time to plant corn in the fields."

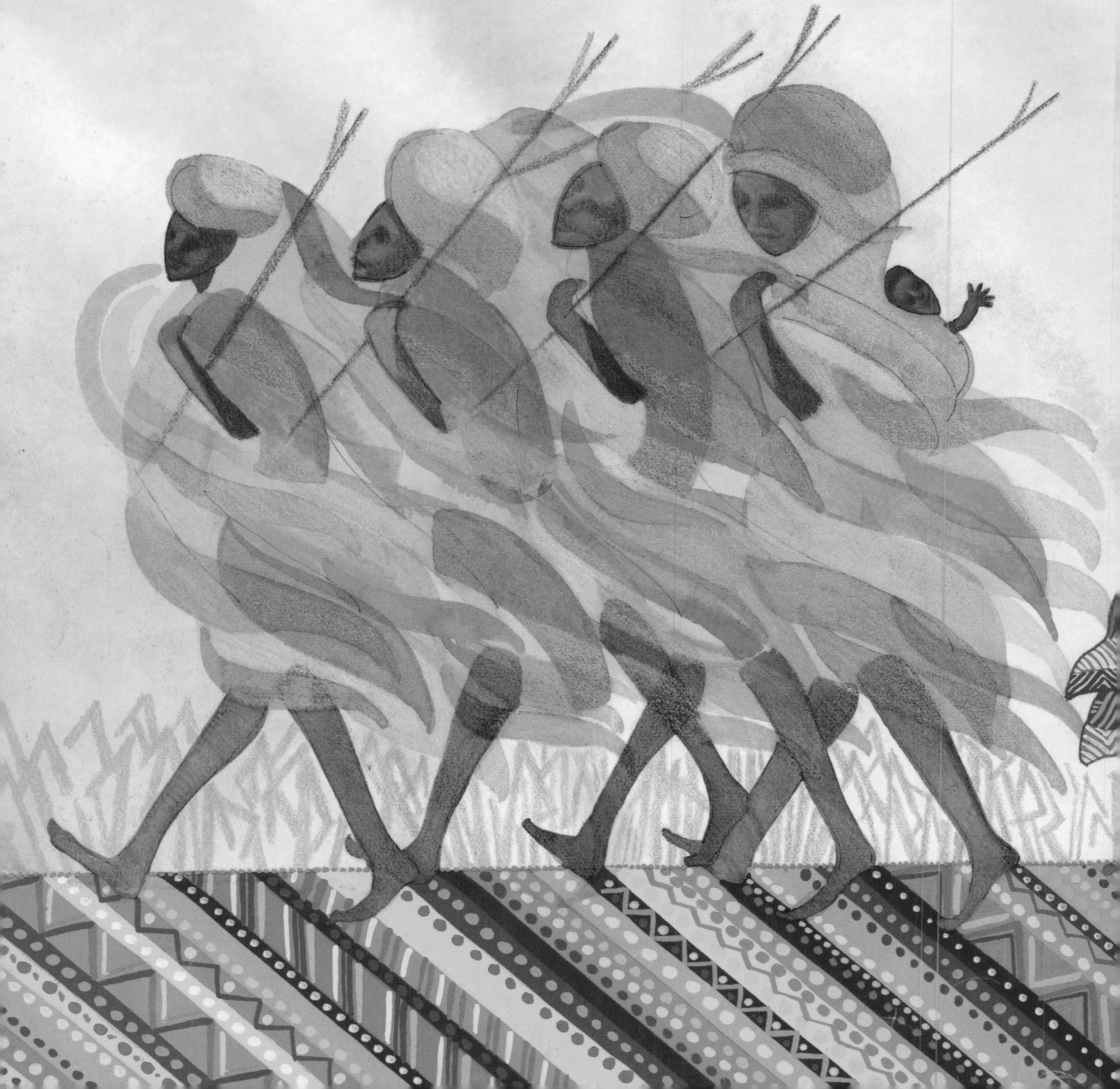

"No, it isn't. I am going hunting in the forest."

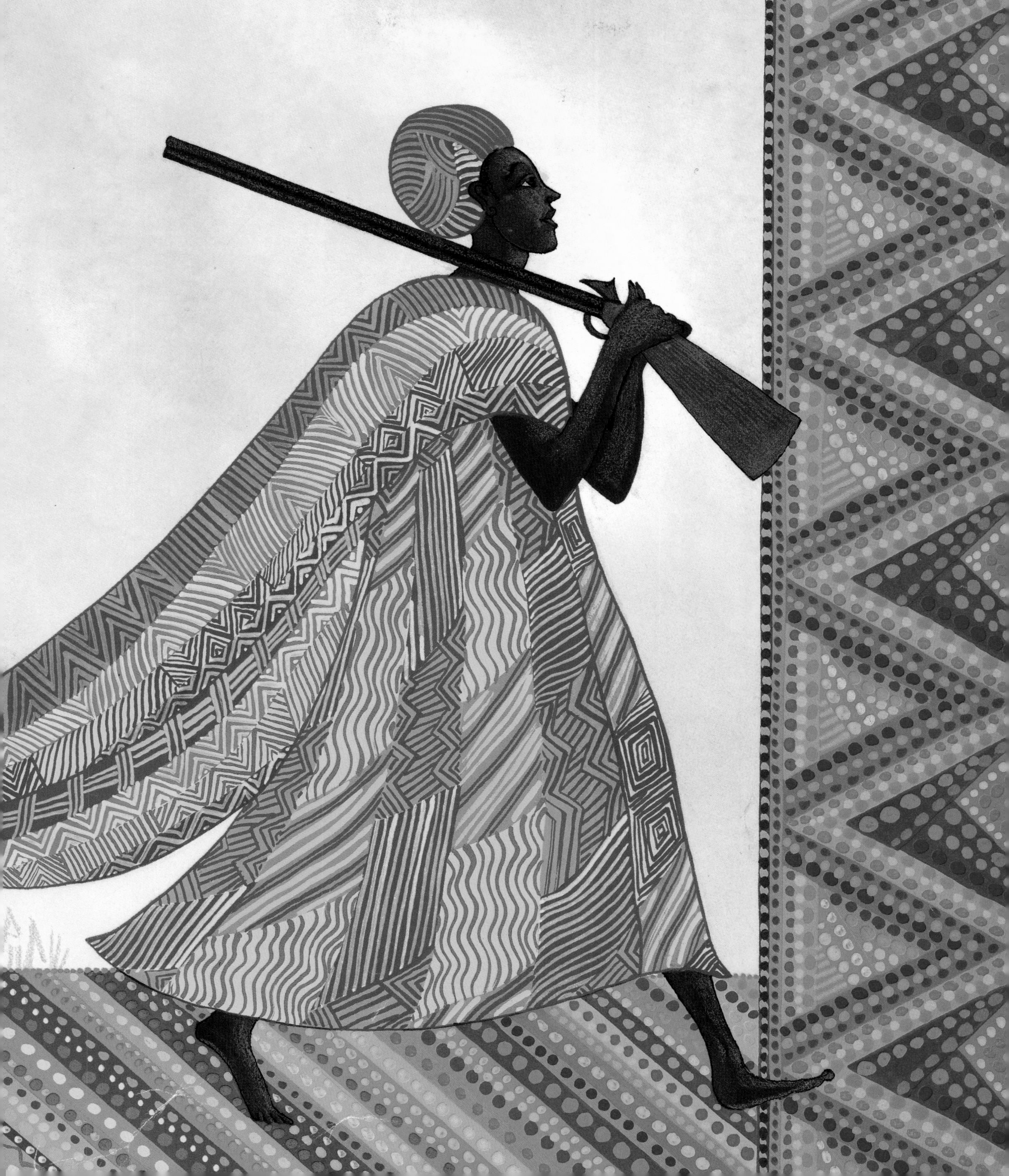

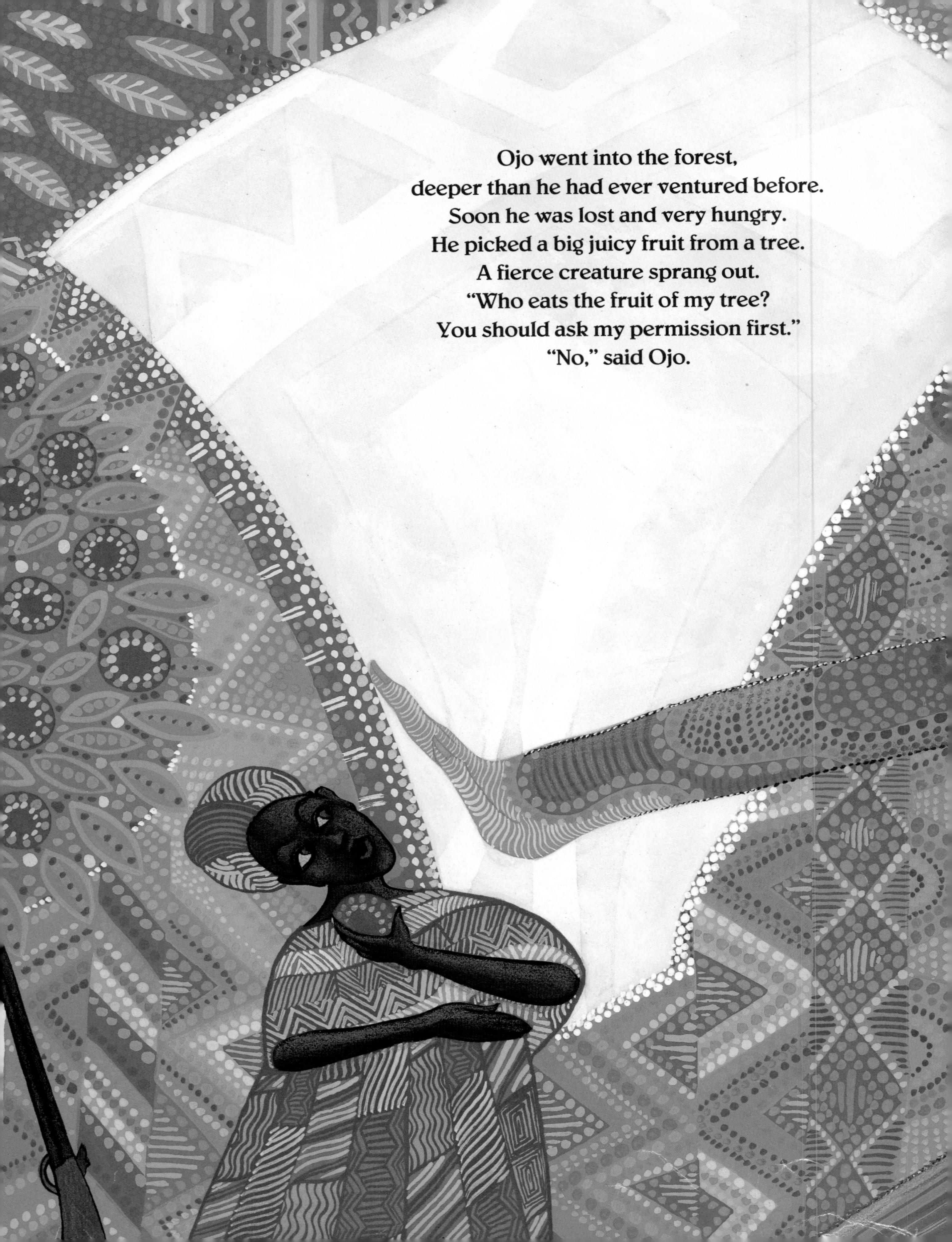

Ojo went into the forest,
deeper than he had ever ventured before.
Soon he was lost and very hungry.
He picked a big juicy fruit from a tree.
A fierce creature sprang out.
"Who eats the fruit of my tree?
You should ask my permission first."
"No," said Ojo.

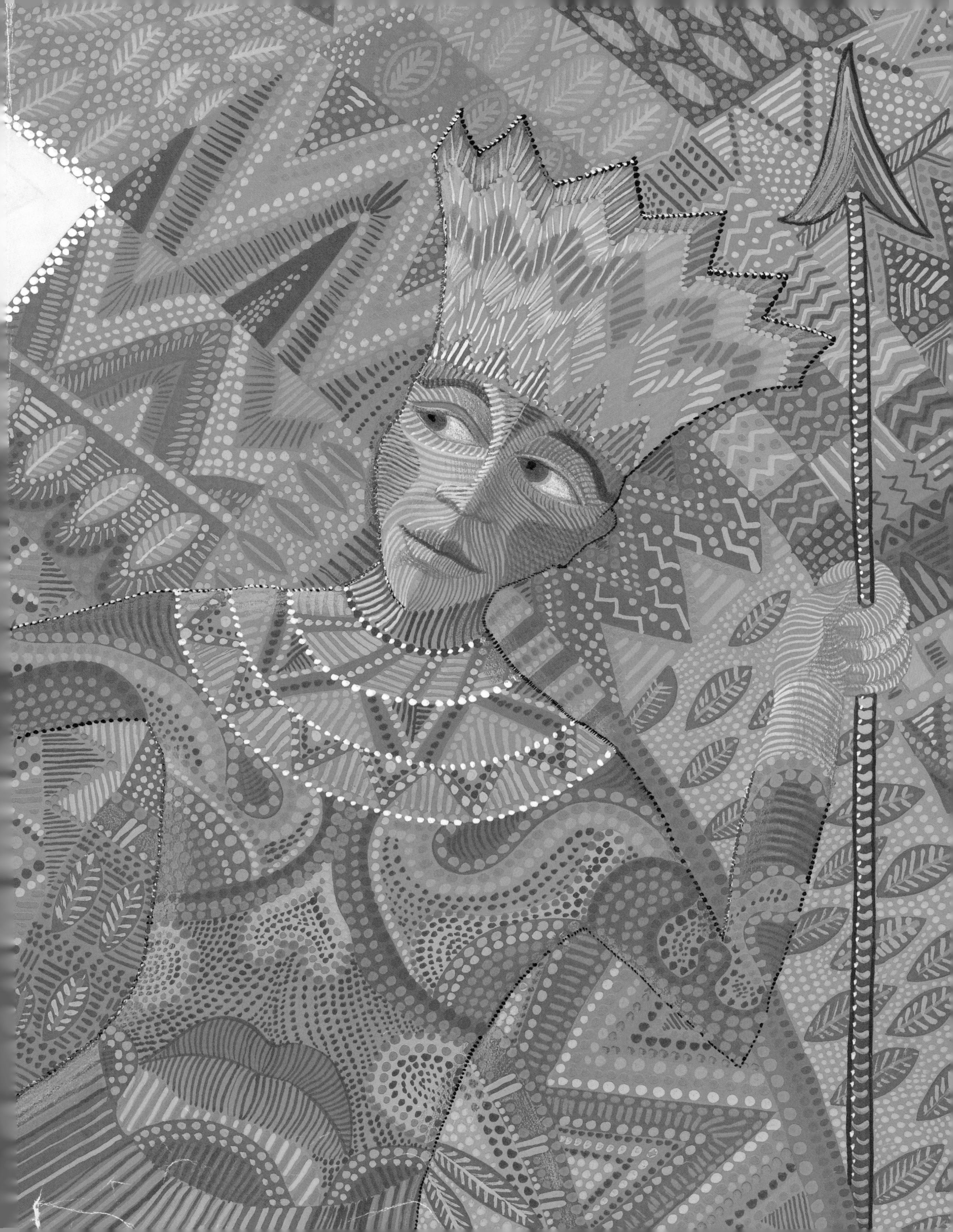

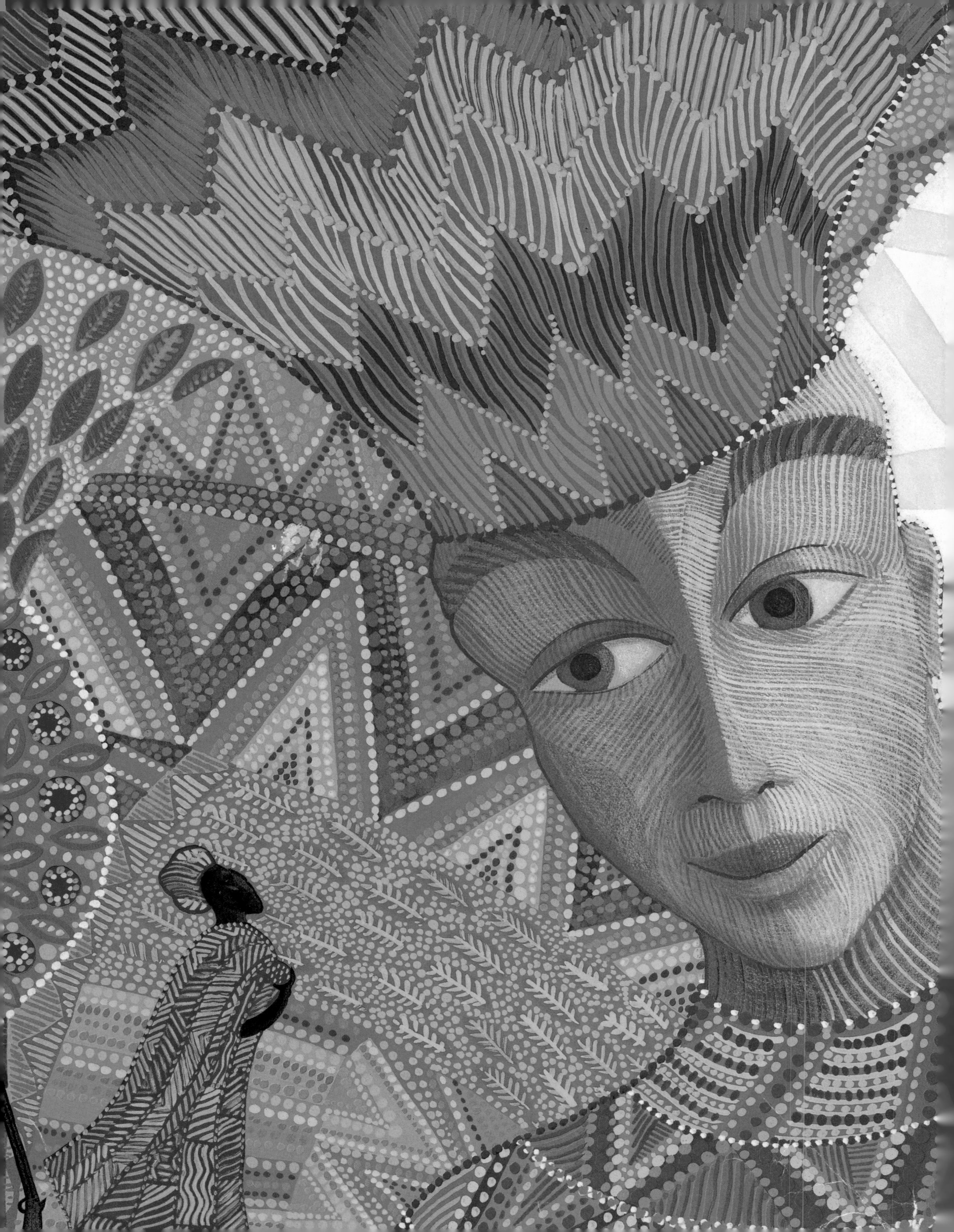

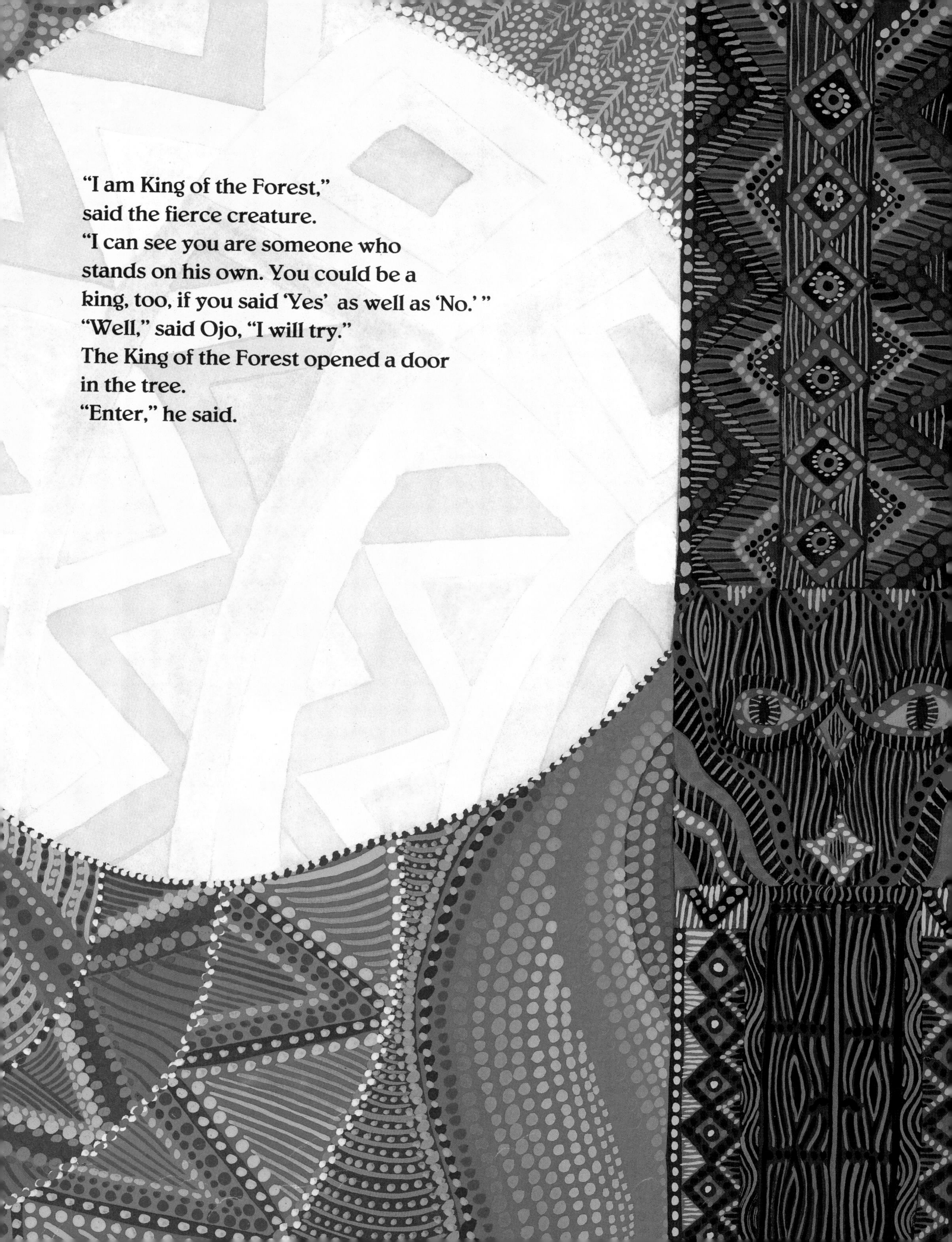

"I am King of the Forest,"
said the fierce creature.
"I can see you are someone who
stands on his own. You could be a
king, too, if you said 'Yes' as well as 'No.' "
"Well," said Ojo, "I will try."
The King of the Forest opened a door
in the tree.
"Enter," he said.

Ojo went through the door
and found himself at the gate of a city.
The people were waiting for him.
"At last, at last, our new king!"
"Yes," said Ojo. He was learning fast.

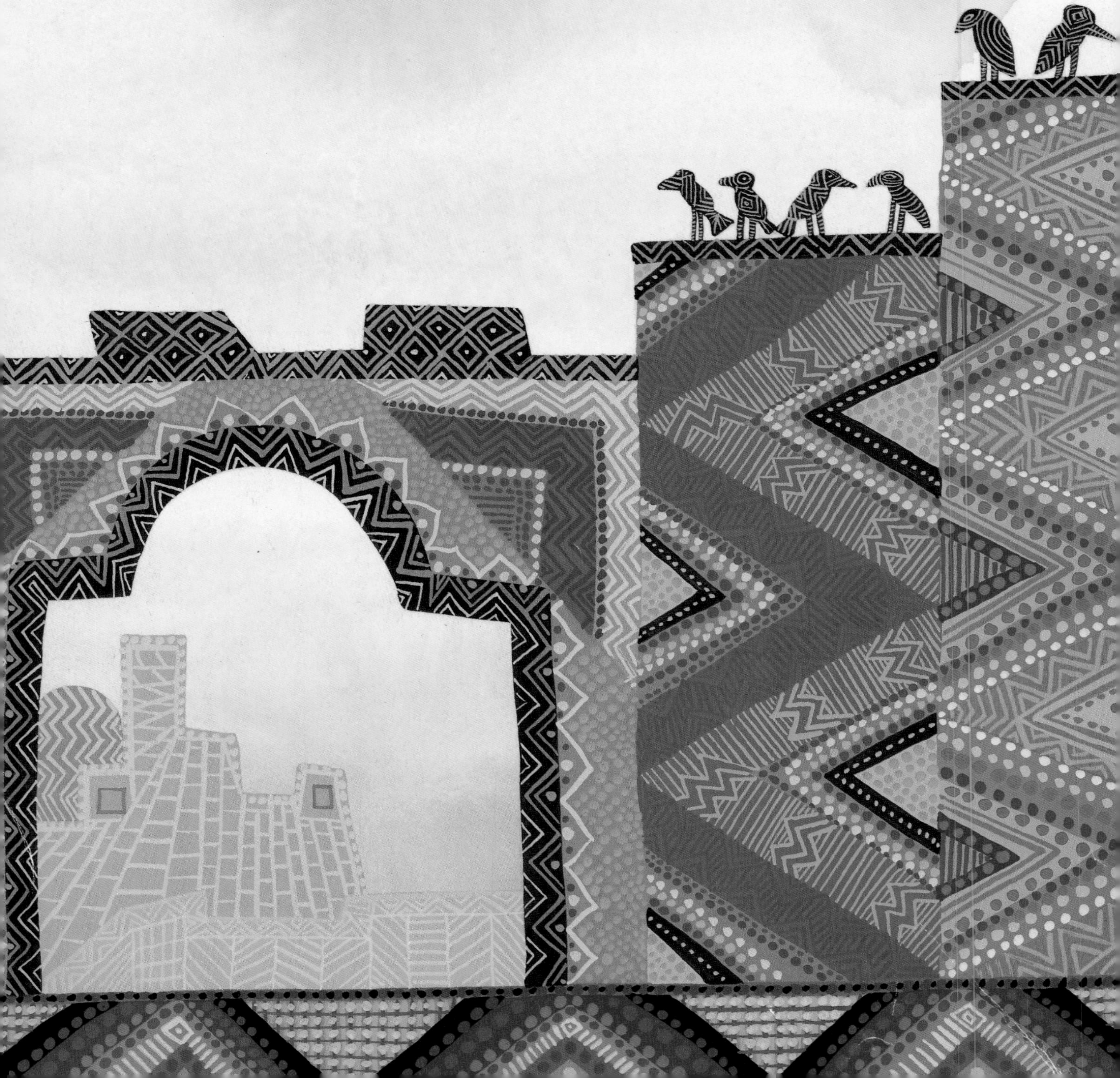

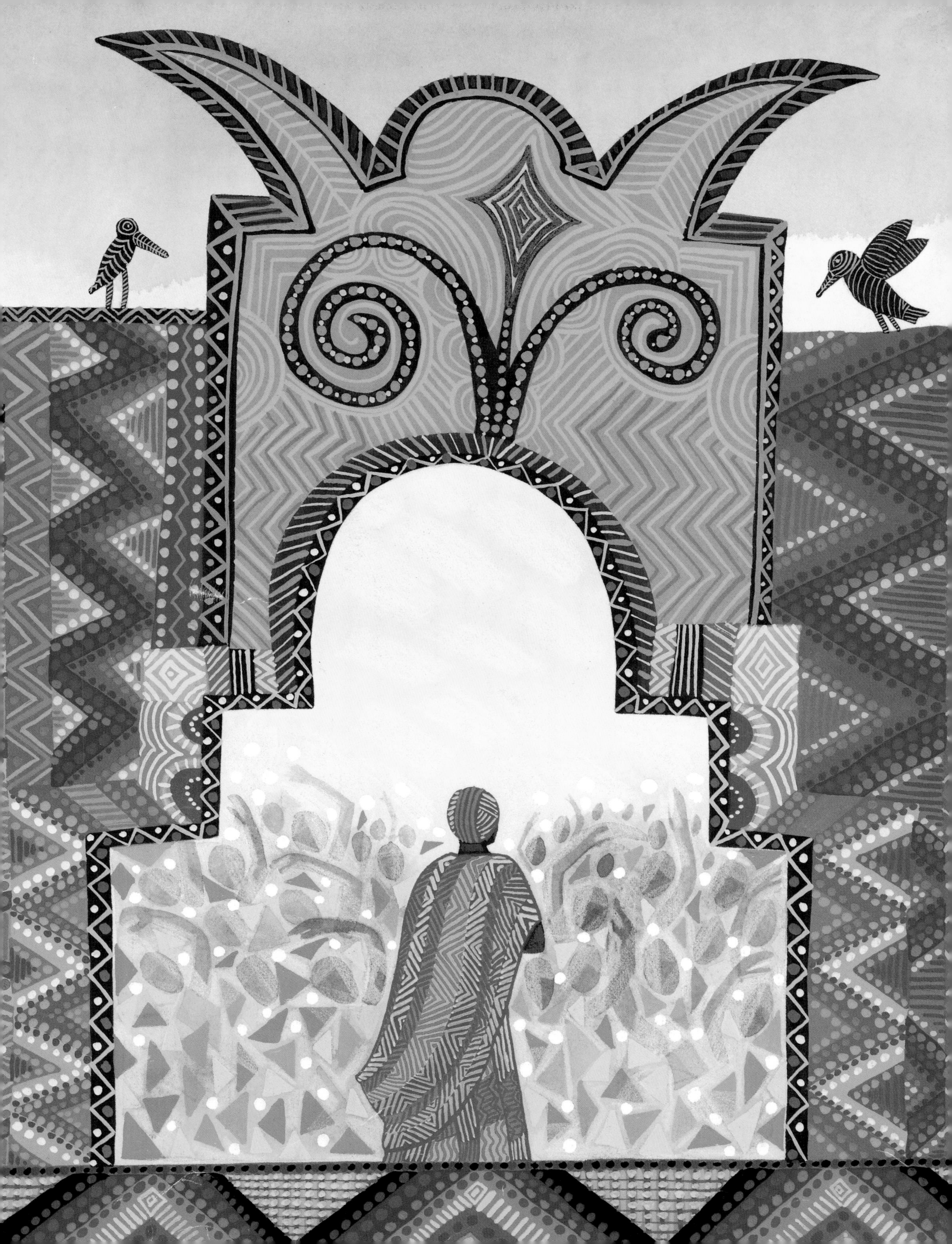

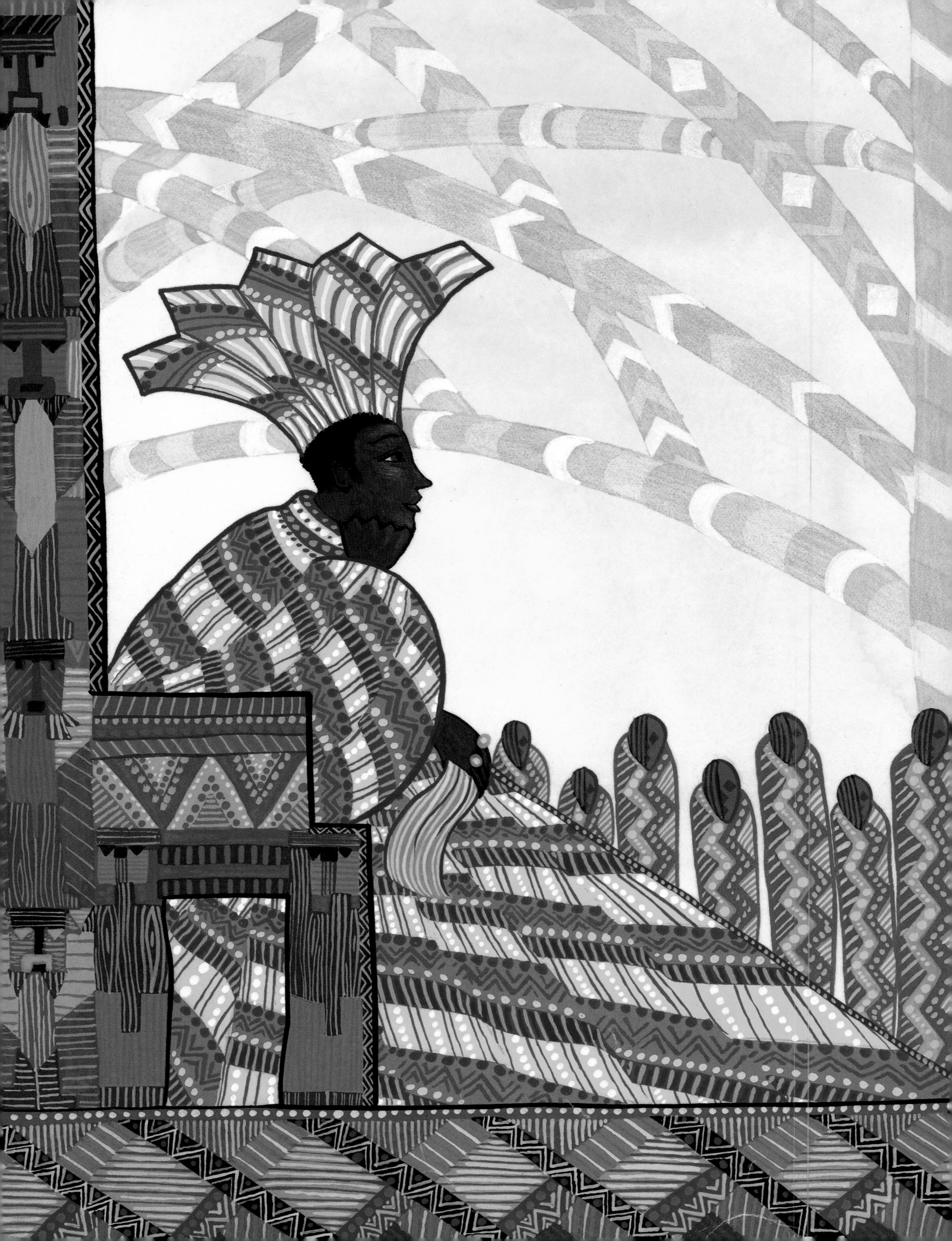

The elders of the city bowed
before him.
"You are our leader. Everything we have
is yours. You will give justice and charity.
You will govern us well."
"Yes," said Ojo.

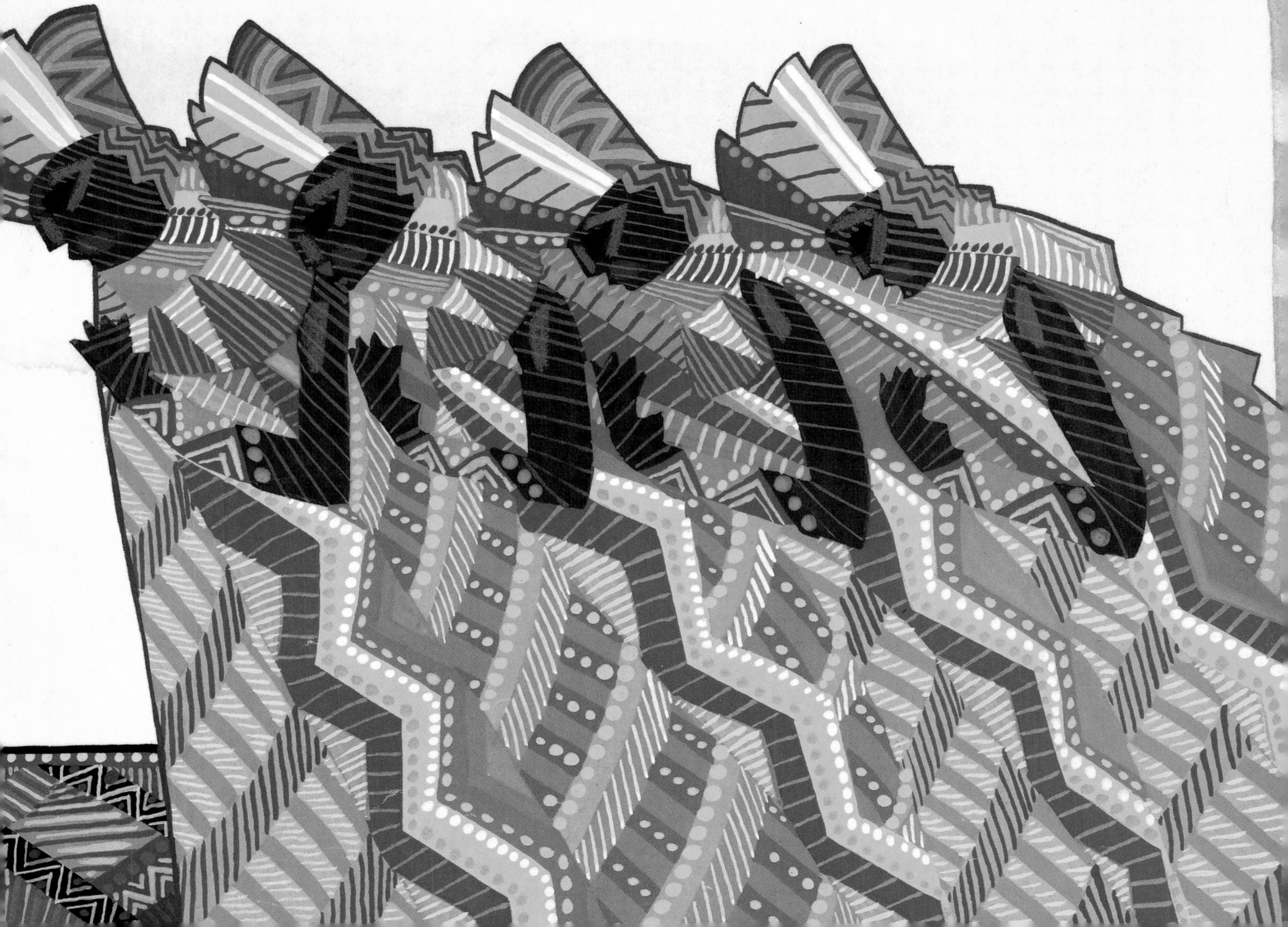

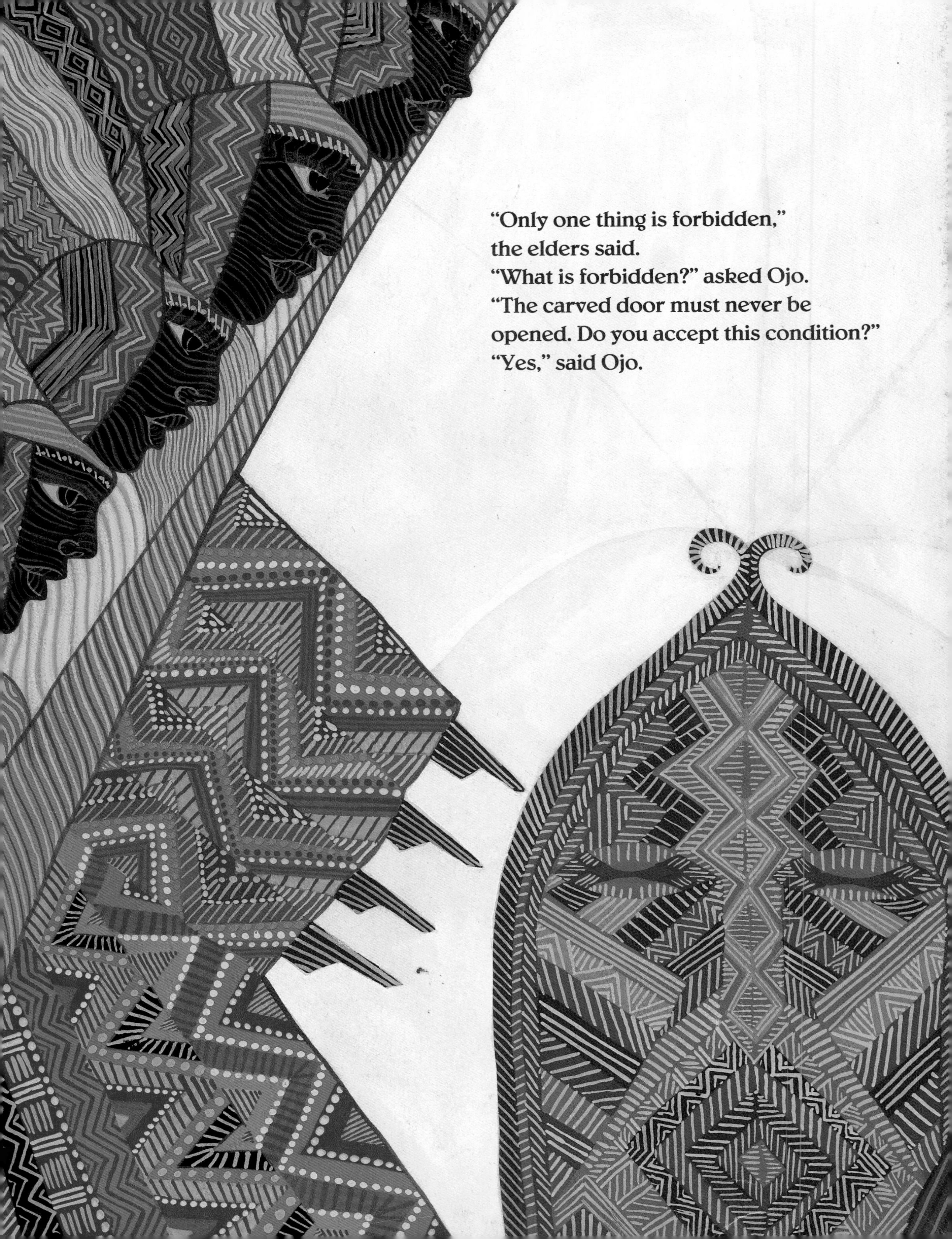

"Only one thing is forbidden,"
the elders said.
"What is forbidden?" asked Ojo.
"The carved door must never be
opened. Do you accept this condition?"
"Yes," said Ojo.

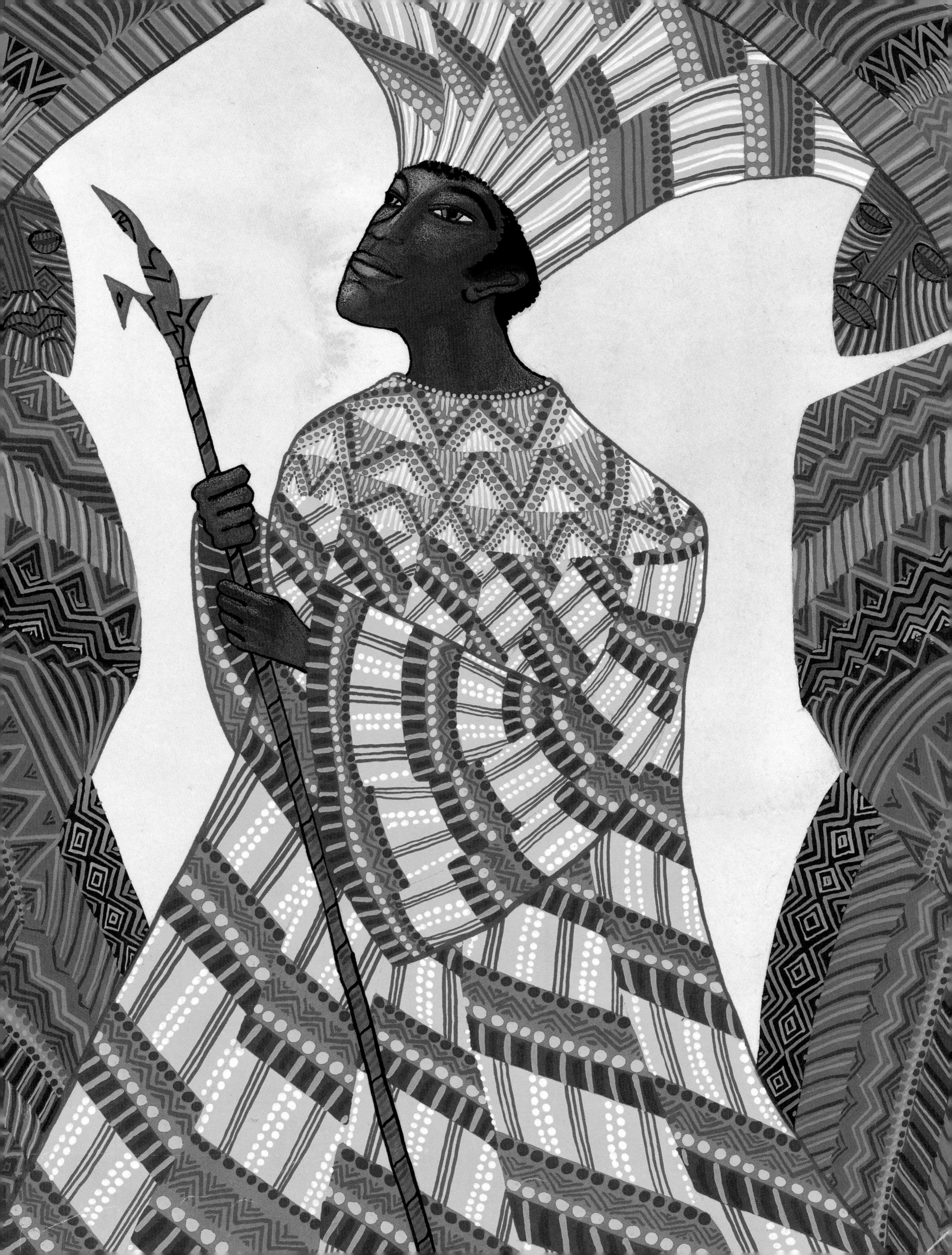

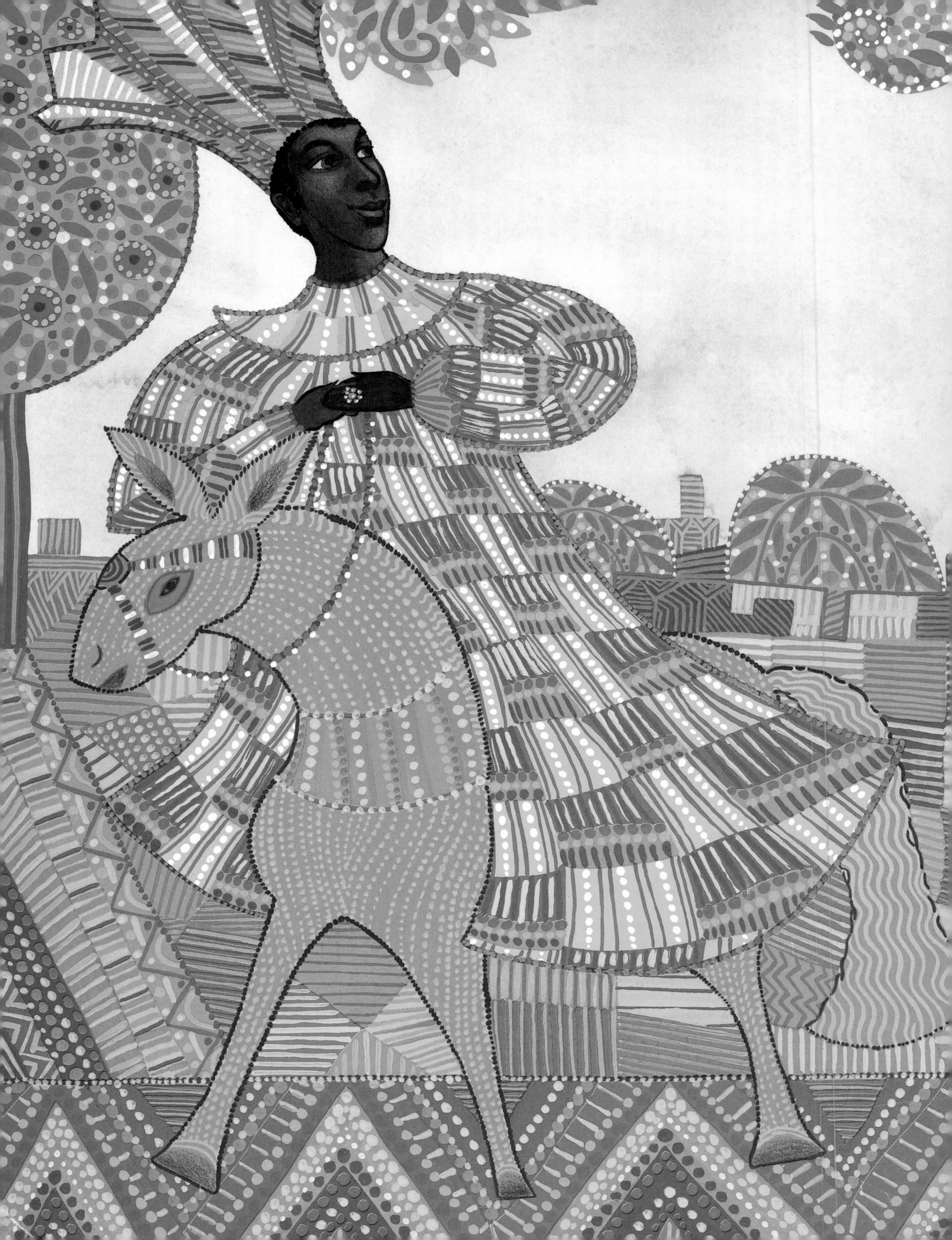

Ojo was a good king.
Poverty left the country.
The tax collectors were fair.
The judges were wise.
Everyone ate well.
Ojo remembered to say "Yes."

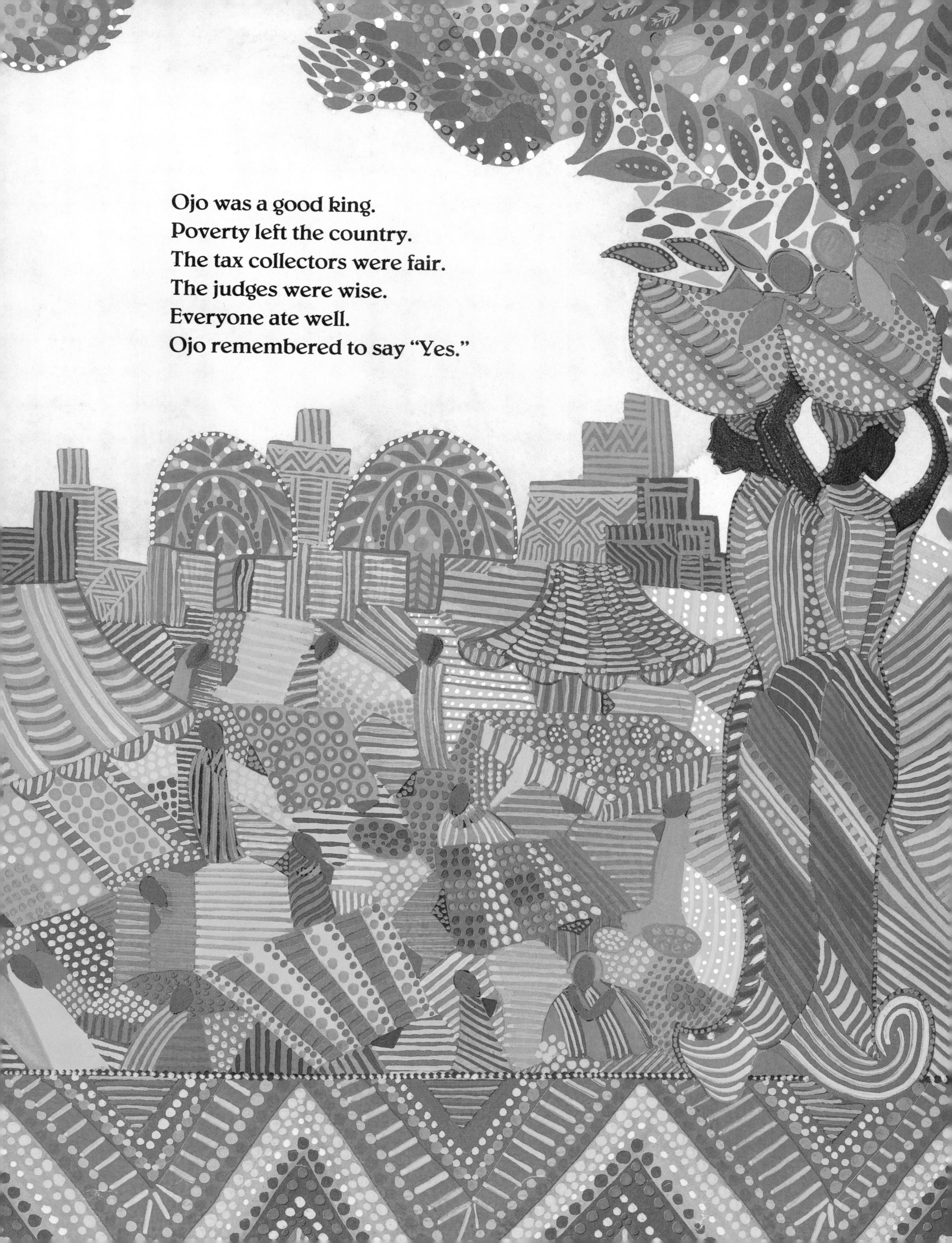

Ojo chose a wife.
She was as beautiful as the dawn.
And she was very happy
because Ojo was generous.
He always said "Yes."

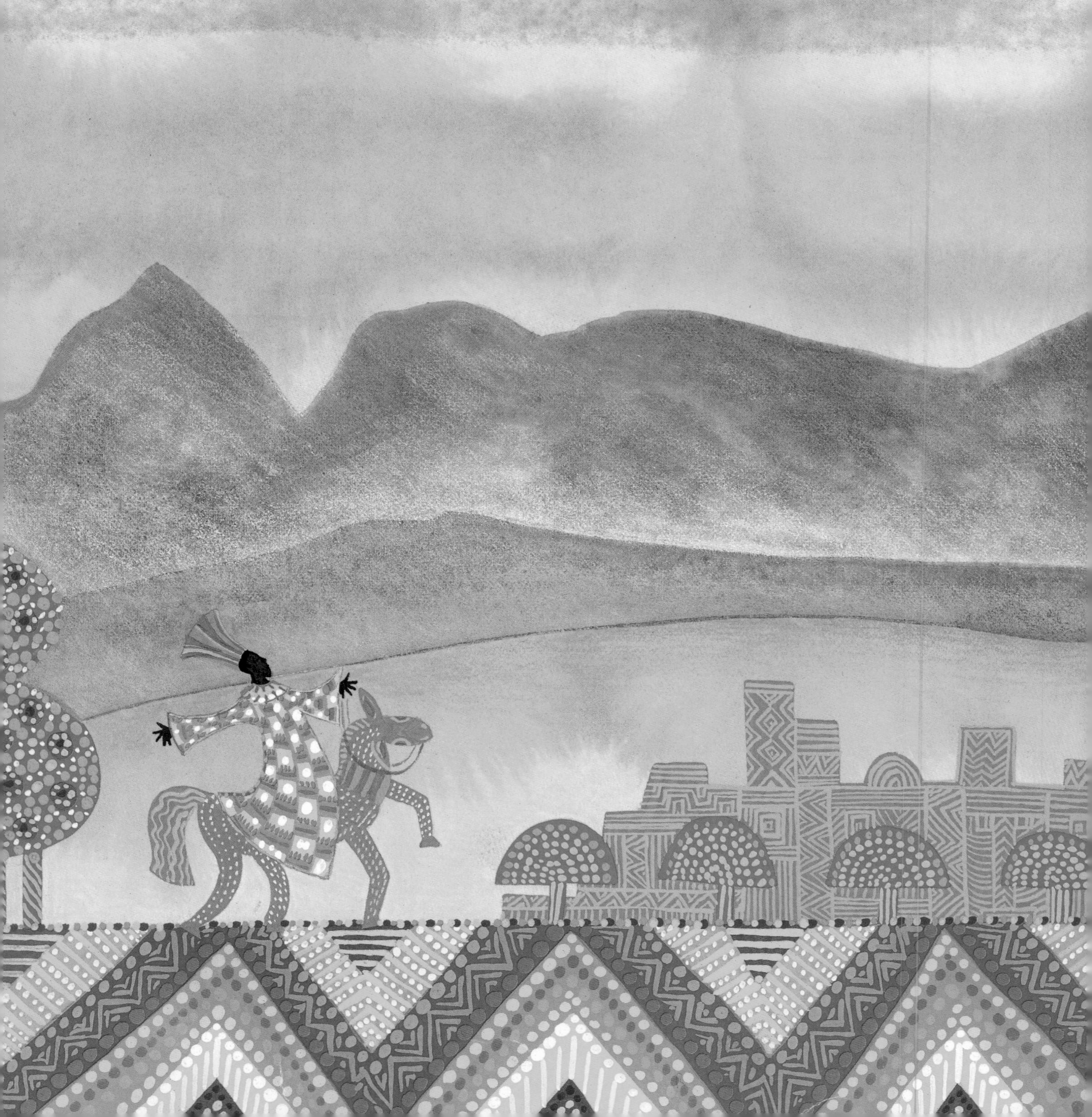

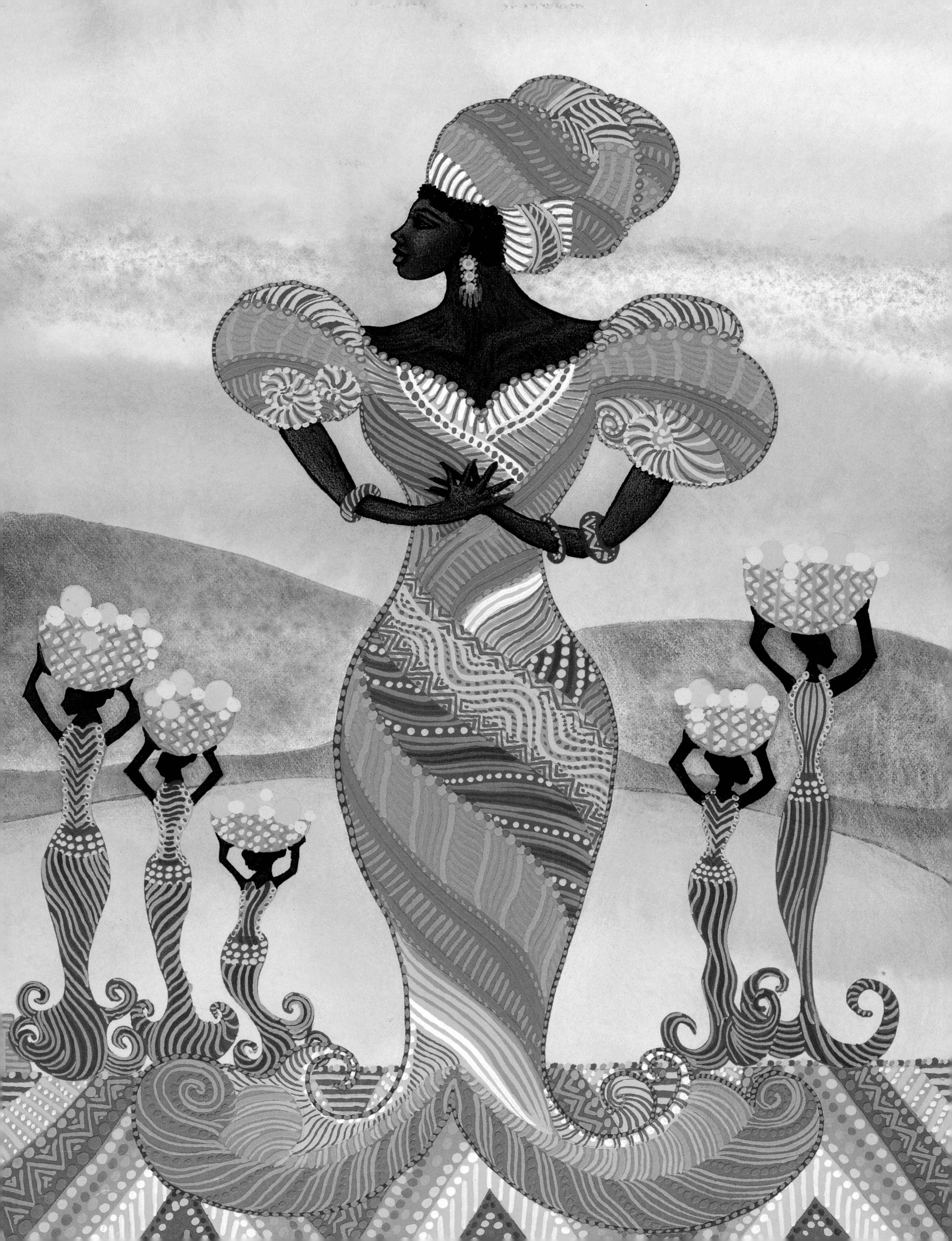

One day
Ojo's new wife stood
in front of the carved
door and said,
"If we could just see
what is on the other
side, our lives would
be perfect."
"Yes," said Ojo.

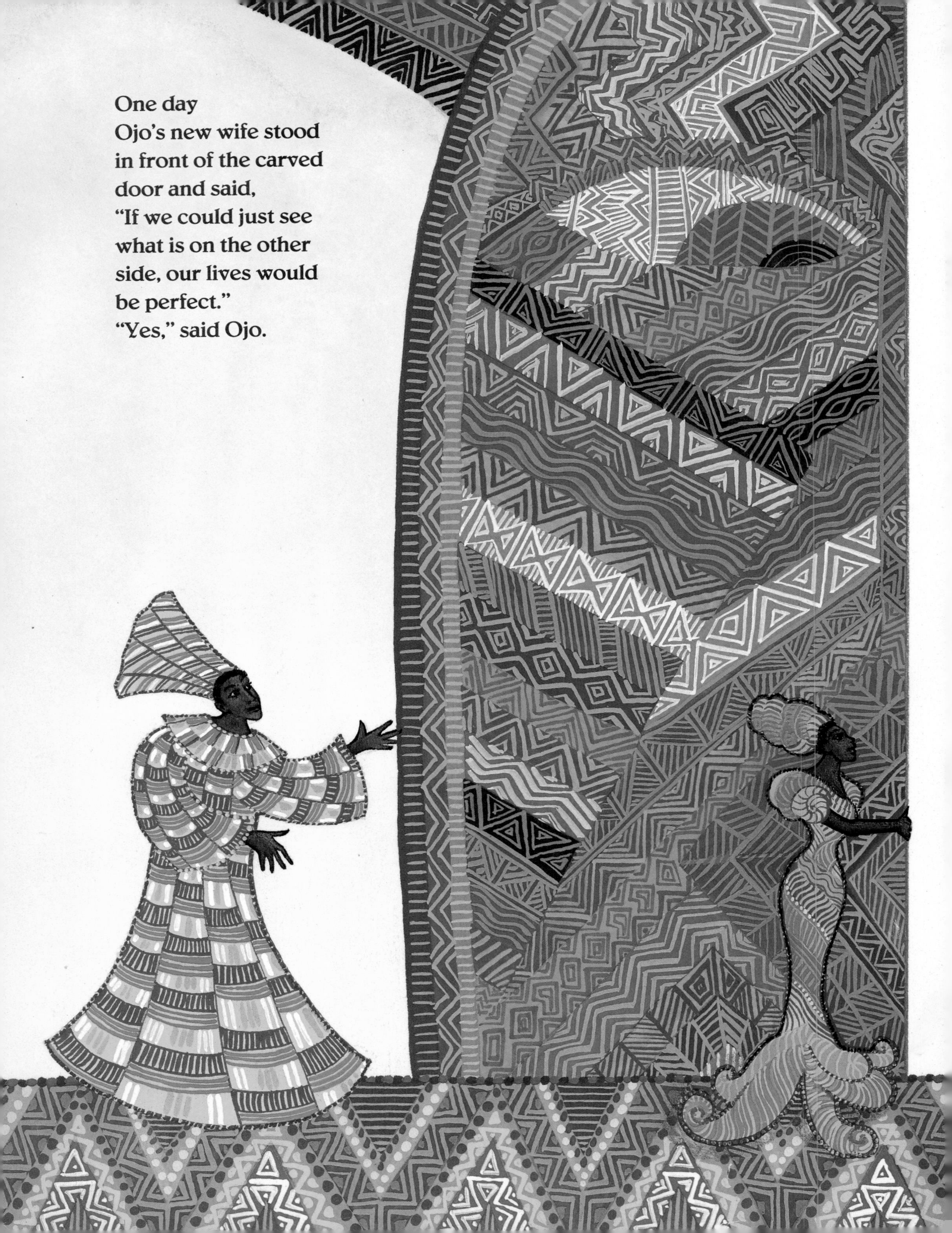

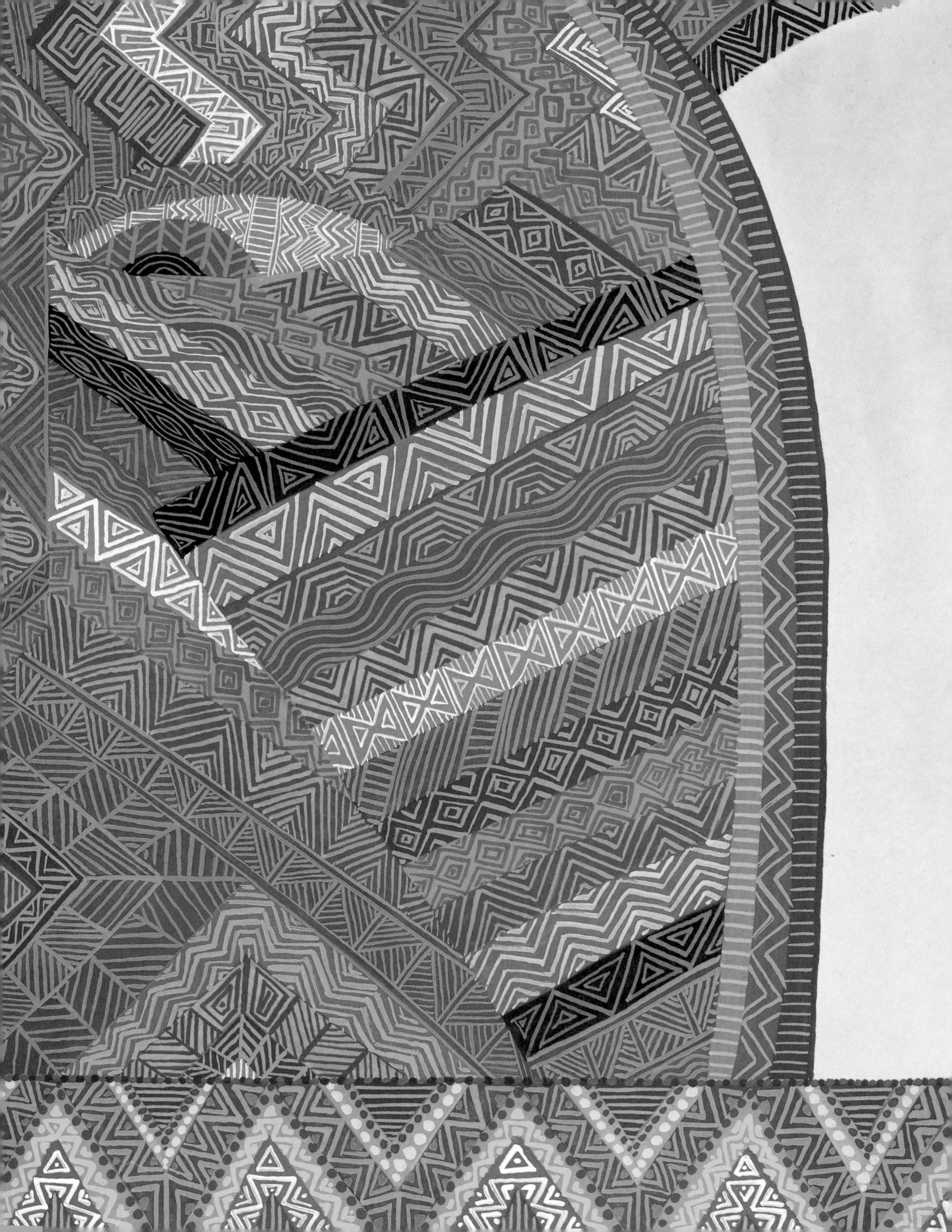

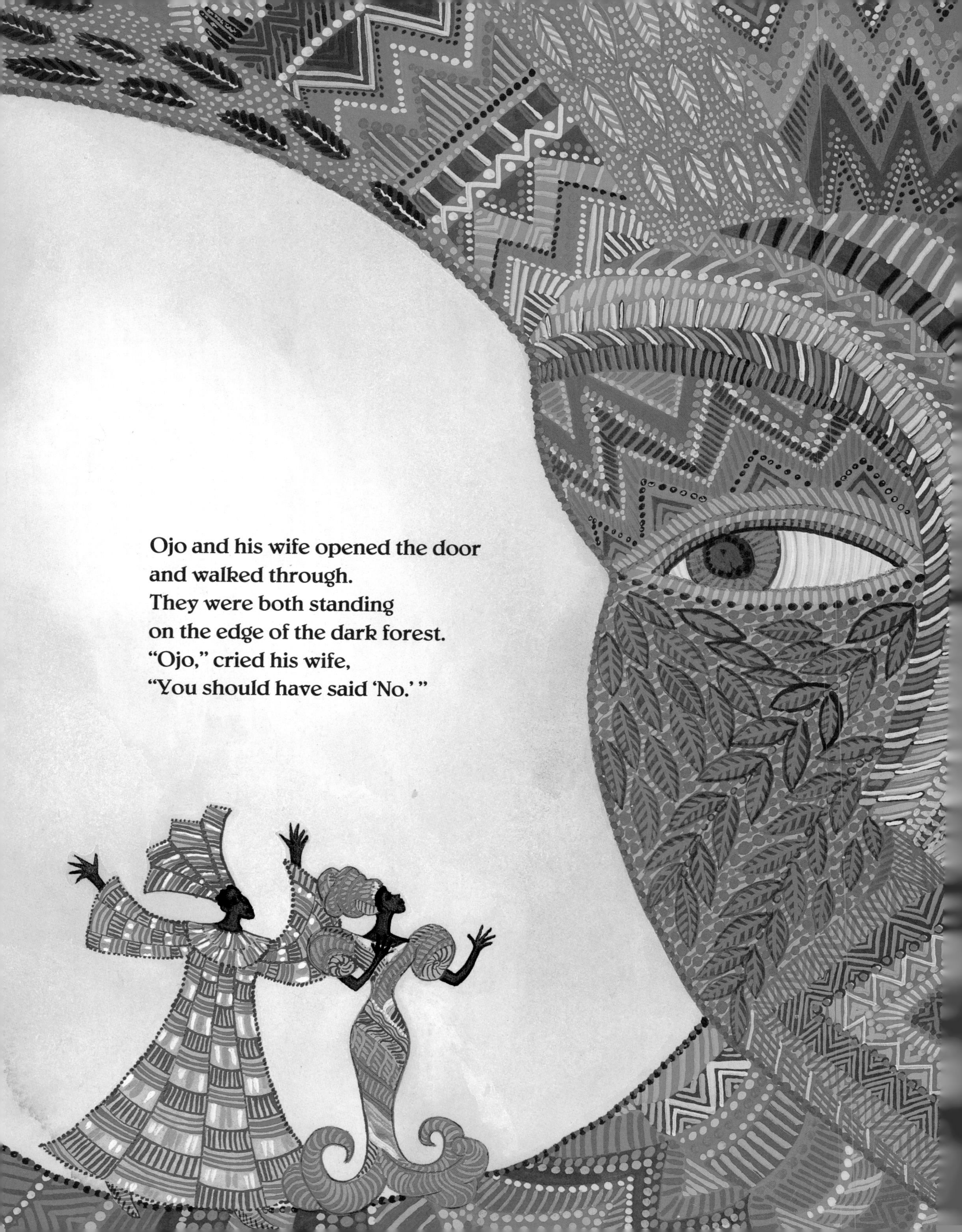

Ojo and his wife opened the door
and walked through.
They were both standing
on the edge of the dark forest.
"Ojo," cried his wife,
"You should have said 'No.' "

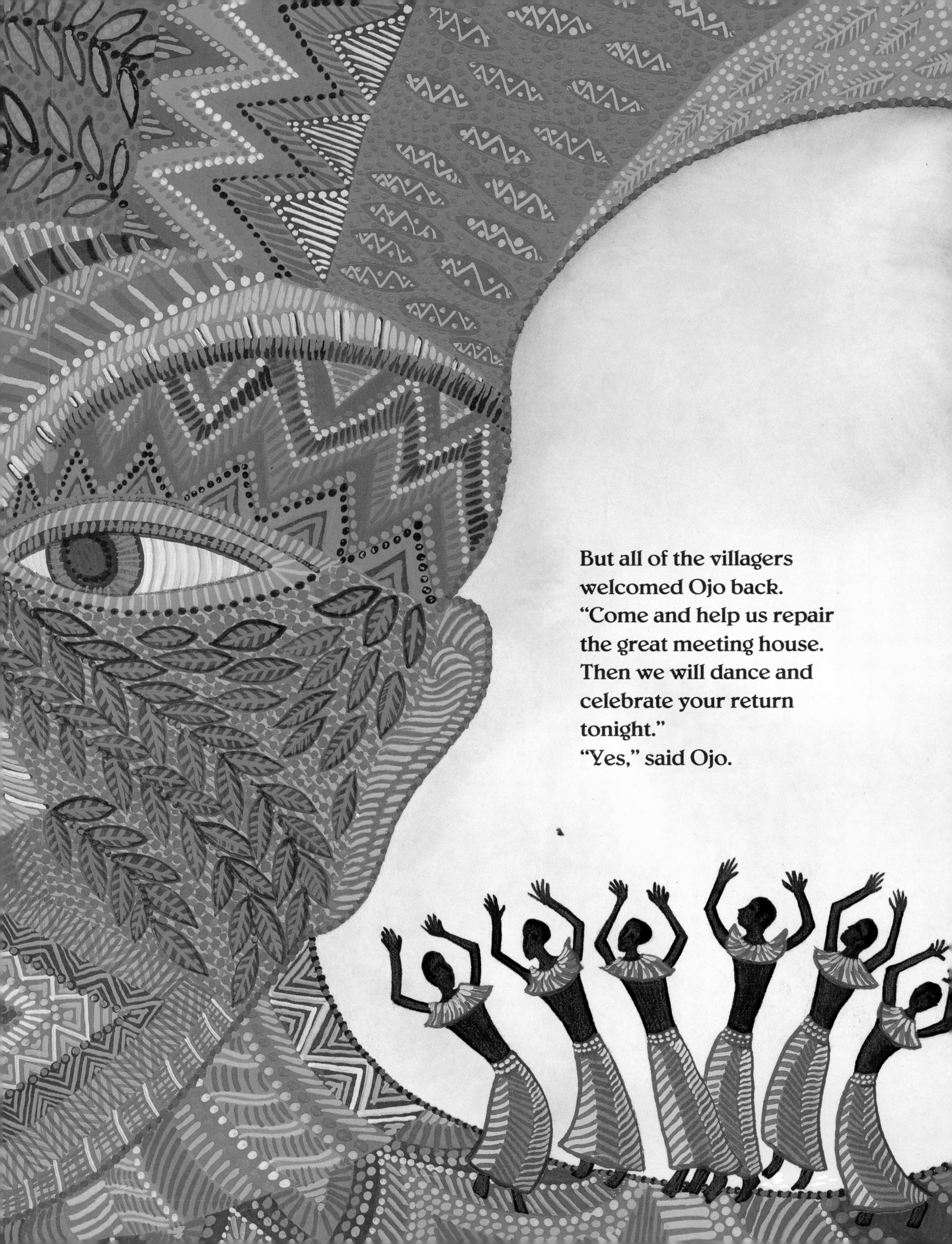

But all of the villagers welcomed Ojo back. "Come and help us repair the great meeting house. Then we will dance and celebrate your return tonight."

"Yes," said Ojo.

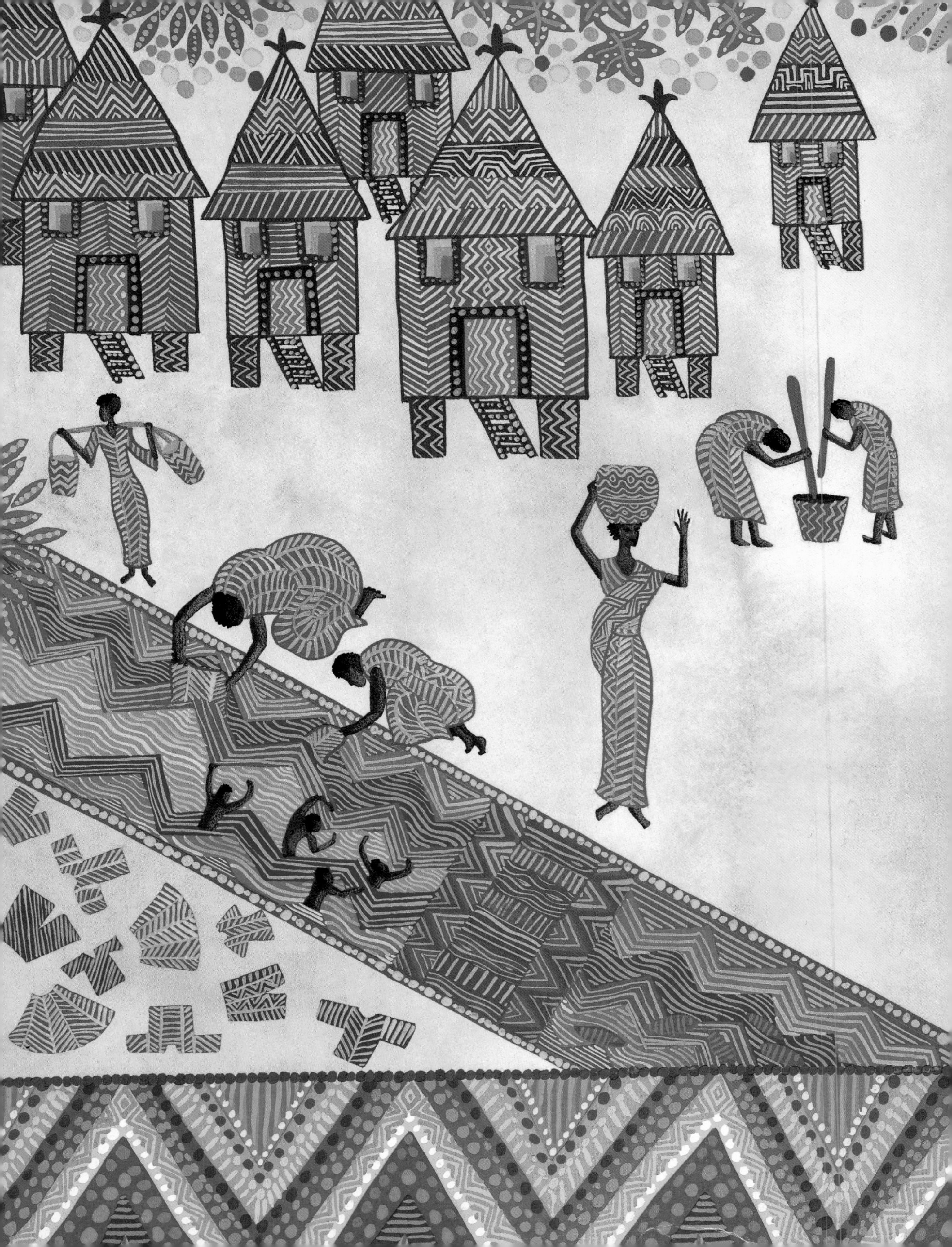

From that time on, Ojo and his wife
lived happily in the village.
He was more friendly with
other people now.
Sometimes he said "Yes."
Sometimes he said "No."
And he never played the drums
too early in the morning.

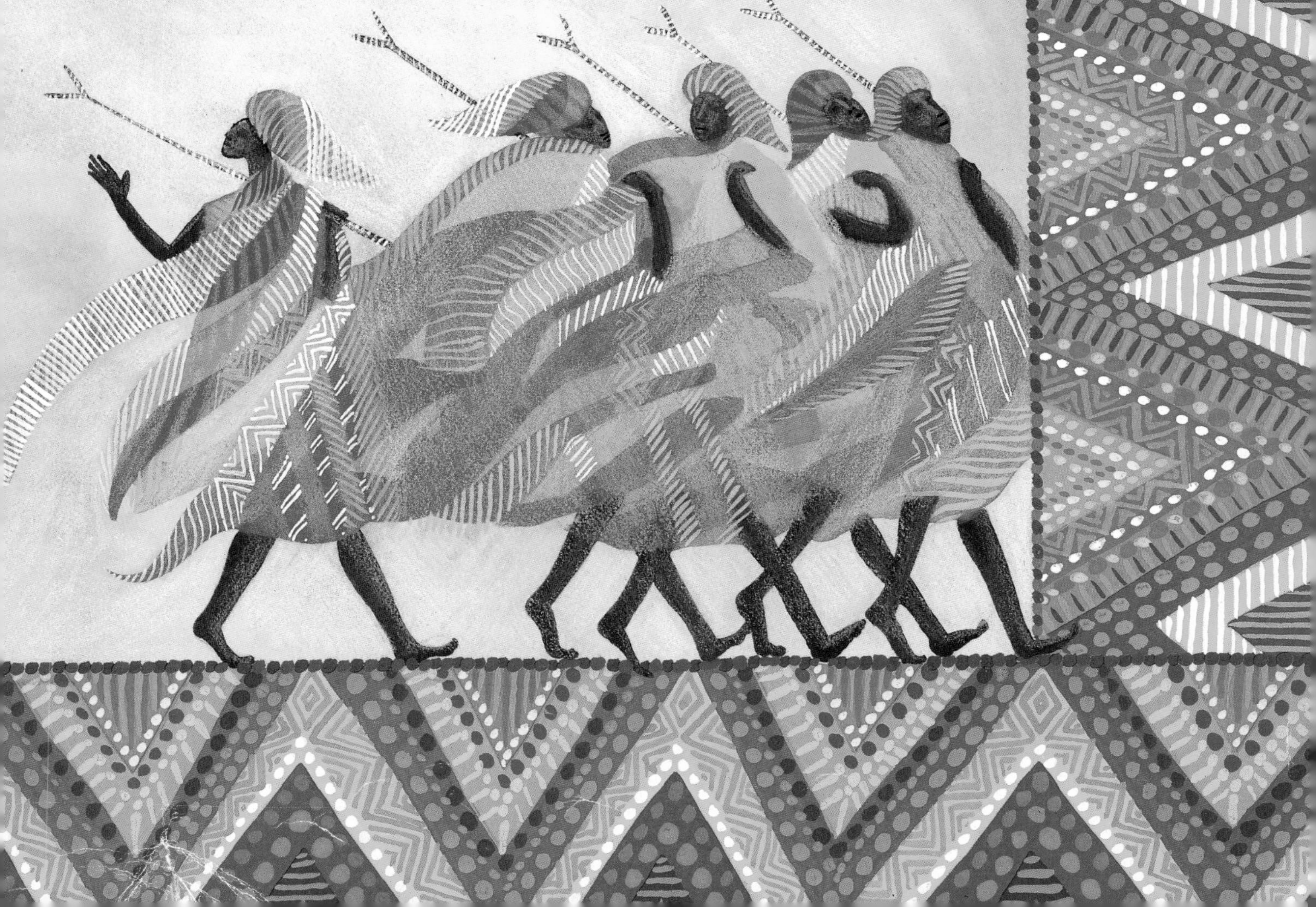